Illustrated by
Laura Chamberlain

Hope the Whale

MACMILLAN CHILDREN'S BOOKS

Once, many years ago, a blue whale was born.
Mother and baby swam and played together,
cradled by the warm tropical waters.

Until spring came, and it was time to
make their long journey together to
the icy waters of the North . . .

The first time I saw the whale, she was far out at sea.
From our small town on the edge of the ocean we would
often see blue whales in the spring.

Today there were two. The little one dipped
and curled, water streaming from her tail.
It was as if she was waving to me.
I waved back. And I called her 'Hope'.

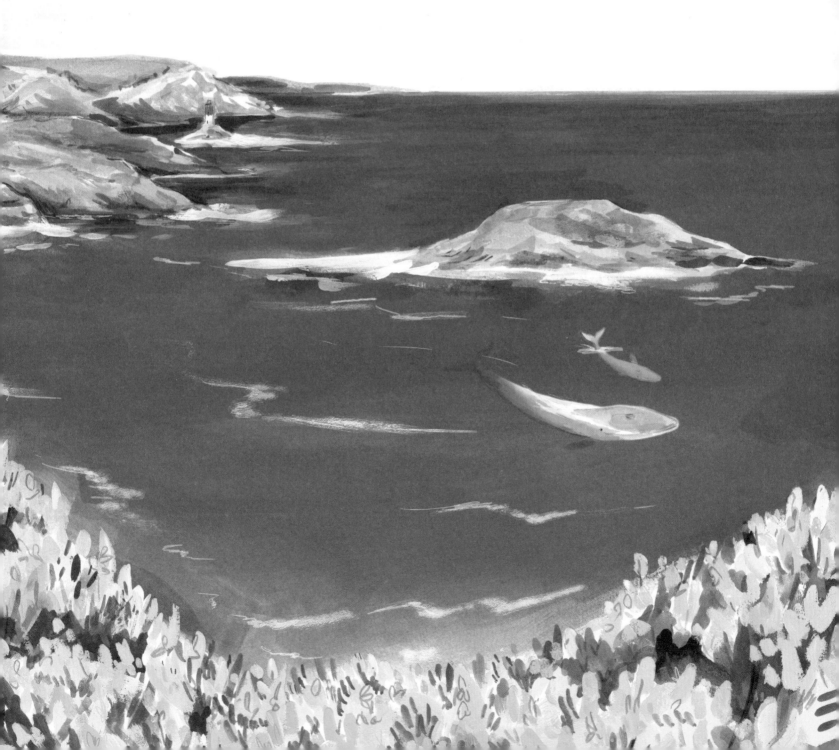

On she swam beyond the bay, following her mother.
I watched until they were two distant specks on
the horizon, heading north.

All that summer long I thought of Hope,
wheeling and diving in the cool blue waters.

I imagined icebergs and polar bears,
great winged gannets and clouds of krill.

Until one day, as autumn blew in and the ice crept
down from the North Pole, I saw Hope again.
Her tail slapped the surface, and she blew
a fountain of water into the sky.

Then she tucked herself in close to her mother,
and the two of them swam past the bay towards
the warmer waters of the South.

That winter, storms tossed our small town on the edge
of the ocean. But where Hope was, the sun sparkled, dolphins
played and people in coloured boats bobbed on the waves.

After the long winter the warmth of spring crept
back to our small town, and with it came Hope.

And so, each year, I'd wait for her.

And each year, as the seasons cycled,
Hope would come . . .

at first with her mother, then alone . . .

mapping across the horizon.

Then, one spring, Hope didn't come.

I stared out at the ocean, willing her to appear.

I went out in my boat to see if I could see her.

I called her name, but she wasn't there.

Perhaps Hope was lost?

I imagined her, far out in the ocean, all alone. Swimming by strange ships, casting shadows deep down below the surface . . .

Hope swimming closer . . .

Something clanking,

something glinting . . .

Then whale song – like a warning. Clicking,
whistling and swooping. And Hope swimming,
powerful. Diving down, down into the depths.
Propelling herself away from the
ship shadows.

And then, one day, I saw two blue whales – a mother and a baby. The mother . . . she dipped and curled, water streaming from her tail. It was Hope! Hope and her baby.

The little whale tucked itself in close, and the
two of them swam past the bay. I watched until
they were two distant specks on the horizon . . .
heading north on their long journey together.

Baby blue whales stay with
their mothers for at least a year,
feeding on milk and growing.
They then start to migrate – often
alone, but also in pairs or small groups,
so perhaps Hope did travel with
her mother.

THE REAL HOPE
THE WHALE

On the 25th March in 1891, a blue whale was found stranded off the Irish coast. Local fishermen tried to save her, but sadly she died two days later. Her skeleton was taken to the Natural History Museum in London, and when she was put on display in Hintze Hall she was named Hope. Scientists have traced her journey, and it is likely that she really did have a baby in the last year of her life. But there is still more to learn about Hope and the lives of blue whales.

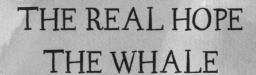

HOPE'S JOURNEY

Hope lived in the North Atlantic Ocean, and every year she made an extraordinary journey, or migration. She would have spent the winter in the warm waters off the coast of Africa, then travelled thousands of miles north every spring, to spend the summer feeding in the rich, cold waters around Iceland and Norway. Blue whales across the world still migrate every year as the seasons change.

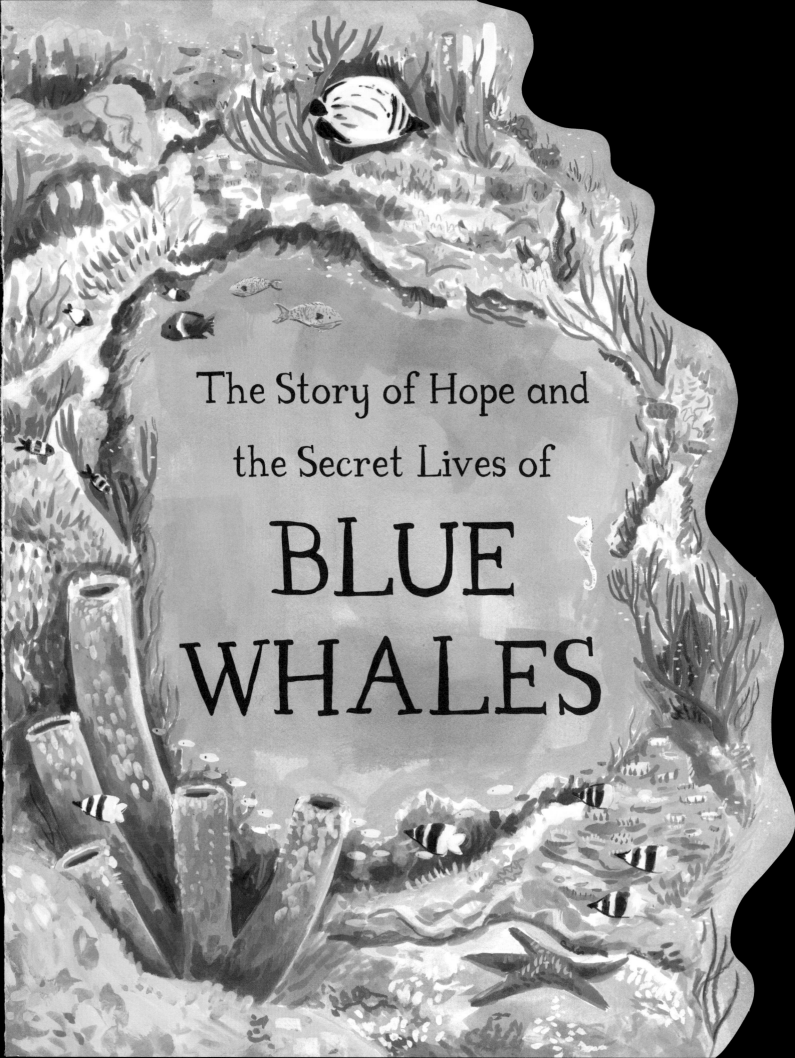

The Story of Hope and
the Secret Lives of
BLUE
WHALES

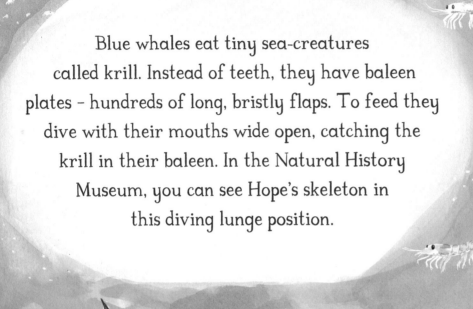

Blue whales eat tiny sea-creatures
called krill. Instead of teeth, they have baleen
plates – hundreds of long, bristly flaps. To feed they
dive with their mouths wide open, catching the
krill in their baleen. In the Natural History
Museum, you can see Hope's skeleton in
this diving lunge position.

Blue whales were
nearly hunted to extinction.
In the 1800s there were an estimated
250,000 blue whales, but by 1966 there
were fewer than 400. That year, people
came together to ban whaling, and numbers
have since increased to 20,000.

But as the oceans fill up with plastic, blue whales are
struggling once more to survive. We can all help by
cutting down on plastic – for example, by carrying a
reusable water bottle and not using plastic straws
or cutlery. Instead use recyclable materials such
as paper. And never, ever, leave litter
on the beach!

Whale song is a strangely beautiful series of clicks, pulses, whistles and moans. No one knows exactly what these mysterious songs are for, but it is thought that whales can hear each other up to 1,000 miles away, possibly using song to warn other whales of dangers.

The largest creatures to have ever lived on the planet, blue whales are up to 30m long, and their hearts alone can weigh as much as a small car. Hope was only 15 years old when she died, but many blue whales live to be 100.

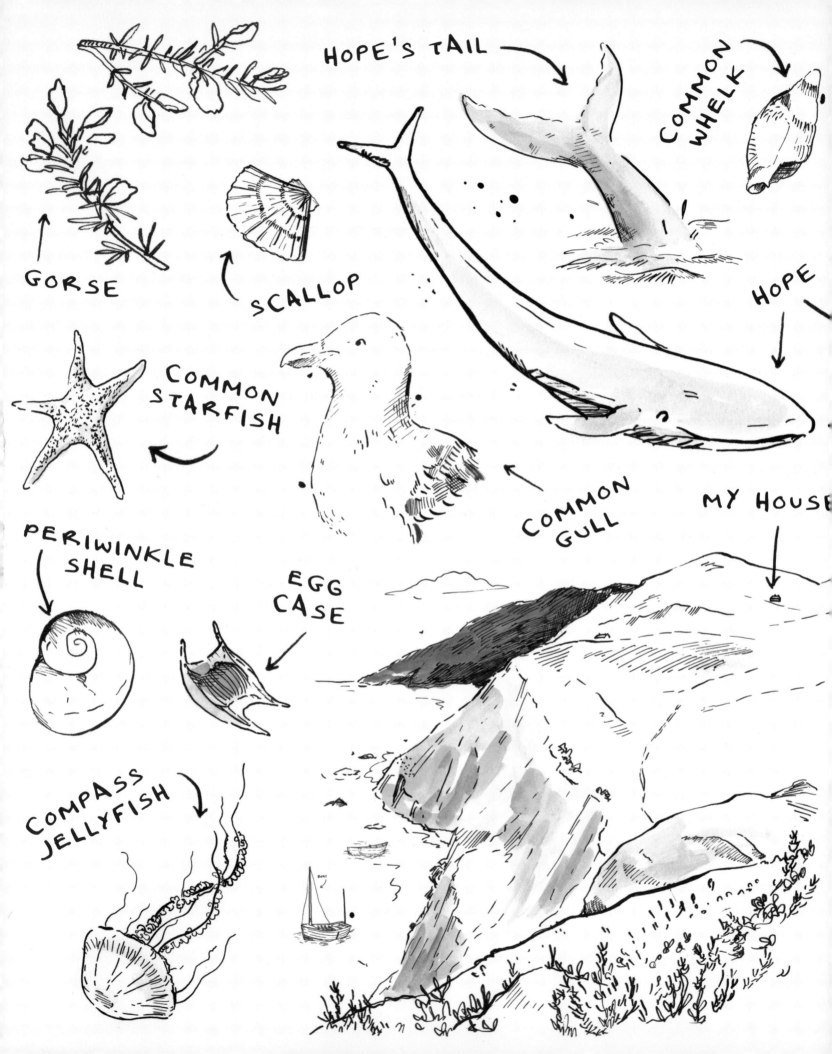

GORSE

HOPE'S TAIL

COMMON WHELK

SCALLOP

HOPE

COMMON STARFISH

COMMON GULL

MY HOUSE

PERIWINKLE SHELL

EGG CASE

COMPASS JELLYFISH